Meet Pippa Mouse—"one of the most appealing mice to appear in recent fiction!"*

"Now tell me the story of Not-Even," says Pippa.
"Who is Not-Even?" asks Mother.
"You know," says Pippa. "Stop fooling me."
Mother says,
" 'Twas the night before Christmas
And all through the house,
Not a creature was stirring,
Not-Even, a mouse . . . !"

* *Psychology Today*

HERE'S PIPPA!

TWELVE STORIES FOR READING ALOUD
OR READING ALONE

By Betty Boegehold
Illustrated by Cyndy Szekeres

(originally published as *Pippa Mouse* and *Here's Pippa Again!*)

Bullseye Books • Alfred A. Knopf
New York

DR. M. JERRY WEISS, Distinguished Service Professor of Communications at Jersey City State College, is the educational consultant for Bullseye Books. A past chair of the International Reading Association President's Advisory Committee on Intellectual Freedom, he travels frequently to give workshops on the use of trade books in schools.

A BULLSEYE BOOK PUBLISHED BY ALFRED A. KNOPF, INC.

Library of Congress Catalog Card Number: 88-27256
ISBN: 0-394-82702-3 (pbk.)
RL: 2.0
First Bullseye edition: July 1989

Manufactured in the United States of America
0 1 2 3 4 5 6 7 8 9

The Stories

To the three cousins—
Julie, Abby, and Felicity

HERE'S PIPPA!

Her *Mouse* House

Rain is falling
outside the mouse-hole house.
Pippa is tired of
watching the rain.
"Mother, tell me a story,"
says Pippa.

"Not yet, dear," says Mother.
"I must make the beds."
"I will help you," says Pippa.

Slip-slap. Slip-slap. Slap-slip.
The beds are made.

"Now is it time for a story?"
asks Pippa.
"Not yet, dear," says Mother.
"Now it is time to sweep."
"I will help you," says Pippa.

Sweep. Sweep.
Brush and sweep.
The sweeping is done.
"Now is it story time?" asks Pippa.

"My goodness!" says Mother.
"Look at the rain!
It is coming right into
our mouse-hole house."

The rain is coming down fast,
making big puddles in the green grass,
and little puddles
on the floor of the mouse-hole house.

"I will shut the door," says Pippa.
"You know we have no door," says Mother.
"Then I will make a door,"
says Pippa Mouse.

She takes some wood
from the big woodpile
and puts it all around the hole
of the mouse-hole house.

Then she takes more pieces
from the big woodpile
and nails them together.

Hammer! Hammer!
Bang! Bang! Bang!
With her strong white paws
Pippa makes a door—
a good tight door,
with a good tight frame
all around.

"There!" says Pippa.
"I made a door!"
"Thank you, Pippa Mouse,"
says Mother.
"Now we *do* have a door,
and we *don't* have puddles.
So now it is time
for a story."

Mother sits in her chair
by the warm red fire.
Pippa sits in her chair
right beside her Mother.

Mother says,
"Once upon a time,
a big brave mouse
found puddles coming
in her mouse-hole house.
She took a hammer
and with Bing, Bang, Bin!
kept all the water
from blowing right in!
Now, who's snug
as a bug in a rug?
Who's the brave dry mouse
in her new-door house?"

"Oh, Mother," says Pippa.
"I know who it is . . .
ME!"

A New Nest

Gray Bird is making a nest in a bush.
Around and around she turns,
making a soft cup of a nest.

"That's a pretty good nest," says Pippa.
"Strong on the outside
and soft on the inside."
"Climb in," says Gray Bird.

Pippa sits down in the nest.
Gray Bird sits down too—
right on top of Pippa.
Under her wings, Pippa is warm—
too warm to breathe.
So out of the nest she climbs.

"A good nest," says Pippa,
"but much too small
for a big mouse and a bird.
Goodbye."

Then Pippa Mouse sees Ripple Squirrel
racing up and down the old oak tree.
Ripple is carrying leaves in her mouth
to make a summer nest
high in the old oak tree.
"Hi, Pippa," says Ripple.
"Come up and rock in my nest with me."

So up the tree goes Pippa,
out on a branch and into Ripple's nest.

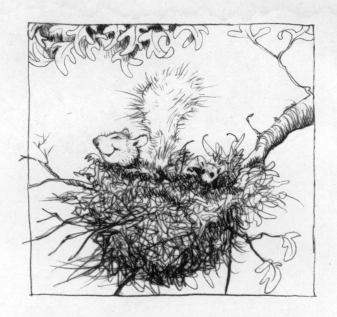

Up and down goes the branch.
Up and down goes the next branch.
Up and down, and down and up
go Ripple Squirrel and Pippa.

"I don't feel very well," says Pippa.
"The ground is too far away,
and this nest rocks too much.
Too much rocking for me.
Goodbye," says Pippa.

Down on the ground, Pippa says,
"I will make a nest myself.
Big and soft and round
and down on the ground.
It will be the best nest
in the world!"

Pippa takes leaves, sticks and mud.
She pushes them and mushes them
around and around.
Then she calls, "Look, everyone!
I have made a nest—
the best nest in the world!
I will sleep in my nest tonight
under the moon and the stars."

"I don't see any stars," says Father Mouse,
coming out of the mouse house.
"And I don't see any moon.
It looks like rain to me."

"No, no, it will not rain," says Pippa.
"Squirrels and birds
are sleeping in their nests.
I will sleep in my nest too."

"Good night then, my nestling,"
says Father Mouse.

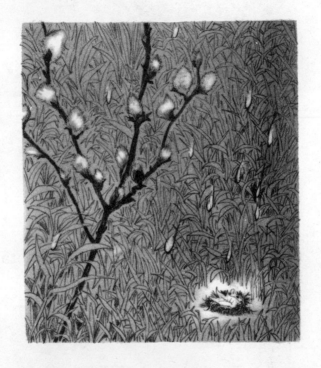

Darkness fills the sky.
Then Pippa hears a little noise—
plop—drop—plop—drop.
Plop-drop, plop-drop.
First one raindrop,
then another.
Now it is raining hard.

Gray Bird puts her head
under her wing
and keeps on sleeping.
Ripple Squirrel spreads her fluffy tail
like an umbrella
and keeps on sleeping.
But Pippa Mouse does not.
She gets wet.

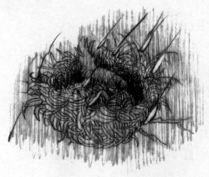

"Who is that?" asks Father Mouse.
"Who is coming in soft as a leaf?"

"Just Pippa," says Pippa,
hopping into her bed.
"Birds and squirrels
can sleep out in the rain,
but a big wet mouse
wants a cozy bed
in a dry mouse house."

Noisy Pippa

Pippa Mouse sits on Weber Duck's back.
Weber is taking her for a ride
across the lake.

"Sit still," says Weber Duck.
"You wiggle too much.
"You will fall off."

"No," says Pippa. "I won't fall off.
I want to wiggle and dance.
Look at the mouse dancing—
dancing on the duck in the lake."

SPLASH!

"Well, anyhow
I had a good swim," says Pippa.

On the shore, Gray Bird is watching a stone.
Halfway under the stone,
a beetle is watching Gray Bird.

"Hi, Gray Bird," shouts Pippa.
"I've been swimming.
Look at how wet I am!"

"Shh, Pippa," Gray Bird says, "be very quiet.
I am waiting for that beetle to come out."

"I *am* quiet," says Pippa.
"Just listen to how quiet I am!
I do not scream or yell or even talk.
I am as quiet as this beetle."

Pippa tapped the beetle.
With his two feelers,
the beetle tapped Pippa, then went away,
back under the stone.

"Oh Pippa, you've frightened the beetle away.
Now you go away too, Pippa Mouse,"
says Gray Bird.
"I don't want to stay here anyhow,"
says Pippa.
"I want to make noise."

Pippa finds a clump of mushrooms.
"Here are my bongo drums," says Pippa.
"Listen to me playing
on my red bongo drums.
Booma, booma, boom!"

"Quiet down there," calls Ripple Squirrel,
high in the old oak tree.
"I am trying to take a nap.
Be quiet, Pippa Mouse."

"I do not want to be quiet,
and I will not be quiet,
and I *can't* be quiet!"
says Pippa Mouse.
"I will play on my red bongo drums.
I will make all the noise I want to.
Booma, booma, boom!"

"Yes, keep on making noise,"
softly calls Red Fox.
"Please make lots of noise,
so I can find you, Pippa Mouse."

Now everything is quiet—
very, very quiet.
Where is noisy Pippa Mouse?
Hiding under a log, she is
quiet as a blink,
quiet as a wink,
quiet as a mouse.

A Good Game

"Come and play with me," says Pippa Mouse.
"Not now," says Ripple Squirrel.
"I must work today.
I must gather nuts."

"Gray Bird, come play ball," says Pippa.
"Not now," says Gray Bird.
"I must work today.
I have to hunt for seeds."

"Weber Duck, you play ball with me,"
calls Pippa.
"No, no! I am working now," says Weber.
"I am diving deep for weeds."

"Then I'll play ball anyhow," says Pippa.
"I'll play by myself."

32

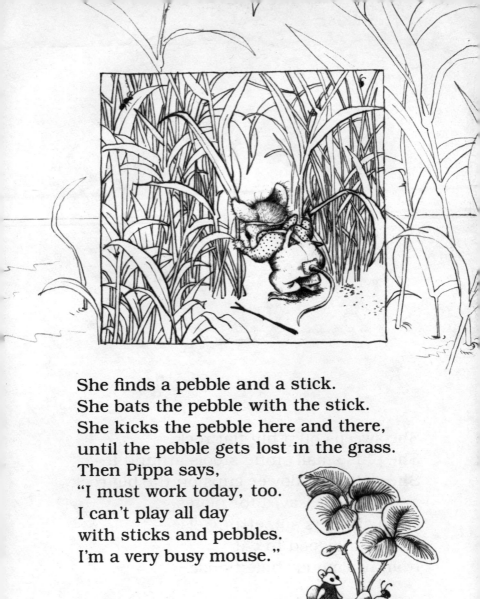

She finds a pebble and a stick.
She bats the pebble with the stick.
She kicks the pebble here and there,
until the pebble gets lost in the grass.
Then Pippa says,
"I must work today, too.
I can't play all day
with sticks and pebbles.
I'm a very busy mouse."

She sweeps off a big flat rock.
She puts small stone stools around it.
She puts four flower cups on the big rock,
and four flat leaves for plates.
Then she gets something else—
something good to eat
from her mouse-hole house.

"Ripple and Gray Bird
and Weber Duck," calls Pippa,
"now you can stop work.
Now it is time to play a game with me."

"I am too busy," says Ripple.
"I am too busy," says Gray Bird.
And Weber Duck says, "I am too busy
and too tired—
too tired to play, Pippa Mouse."

"You will not be too tired for this game,"
says Pippa.
"For this game is called
Everybody-Sit-Down-and-Eat!"

"I am not too busy at all," says Gray Bird,
flying to the big flat stone.
"I am not too tired after all," says Weber,
waddling over on his flat yellow feet.
"I will play this game," says Ripple Squirrel.
"I will play this game with you right now!"

"It is a good game," says Pippa,
"because nobody loses,
everybody wins!"

Ice Mice

Pippa looks at the puddle.
It is shiny and still.
Pippa jumps on the puddle,
and crinkles it all to bits.
"Hurray! It's ice!" yells Pippa.
"Let's go skating, Weber Duck."

"Don't be silly," says Weber.
"My webbed feet are for swimming,
not for skating."

"How about you, Gray Bird?"
calls Pippa.
"Will you go skating with me?"

"Not I," says Gray Bird.
"My feet are too curly for skating."

Then Ripple Squirrel says,
"I'll come with you, Pippa.
If you will try, I will try."

Down on the gray lake ice,
Ripple and Pippa
go sliding.
First on four feet,
then on two feet,
then—BUMP—on no feet!

"If at first you don't succeed,"
says Pippa, "try, try again.
Let's find some skates."

Scribble, scrabble! Scratch and hunt.
They find eight smooth stones—
one for each of their eight little paws.
They hold the stones in their paws
and push off over the ice.

"Look at my skates!" calls Pippa.
"I have four skates,
and I am skating!"

Then out go Pippa's feet
and down goes Pippa.
And down goes Ripple Squirrel
right on top of Pippa!

"I have four feet and
they go four ways," says Pippa.
"So do I," says Ripple.
"Let's try again."

Scribble, scrabble! Scratch and hunt.
They find some peelings of bark
from the big white birch tree.

"We do not have ice skates," says Pippa.
"We have iceboats instead.
We will slide across the ice
on our birch-bark sleds."

Ripple Squirrel sits on her sled
and holds up her tail for a sail.
Pippa Mouse sits
on her birch-bark sled
and holds up a dry birch leaf
fastened to the mast of her tail.

An icy wind begins to blow
across the lake,
pushing Ripple and Pippa
over the dark lake ice.
"Hurray!" calls Pippa.
"Here we go on our iceboats
over the icy sea."

"I will call my iceboat *Sailor Squirrel*,"
says Ripple,
blowing along like a leaf.

"And I will call my boat *Ice Mice*,"
says Pippa,
sailing along beside her.
"*Ice Mouse*, you mean," says Ripple.
"No," says Pippa.
"For I will get my father and my mother
and give them a ride this very afternoon!"

"Hurray, sing hurray,
for the three brave mice!
Who'll sail far away
on the dark gray ice?
Who'll sail the *Ice Mice*
so far out to sea?
Mother, Father and Captain—
and the captain is ME!"

Not-Even, a Mouse

Christmas time is here.
Pippa Mouse wants
to hang up a Christmas stocking.

"But we don't have any stockings,"
says Mother.
"Then I will hang up something else,"
says Pippa.
"What can I hang up?"

47

Pippa looks and looks.
Mother looks too.

"There is nothing else to hang up,"
says Mother.
"Yes there is," says Pippa.
"I will hang up my swimming cap.
It is big and round.
It will hold more than a stocking—
much, much more."

"That looks very funny," says Mother.
"No, that looks very good," says Pippa.
"Now tell me the story of Not-Even."
"Who is Not-Even?" asks Mother.
"You know," says Pippa.
"Stop fooling me."

Mother says,
" 'Twas the night before Christmas
And all through the house,
Not a creature was stirring,
Not-Even, a mouse . . . !

"Now be like Not-Even,
and go to sleep,
for tomorrow is Christmas Day,"
says Mother.

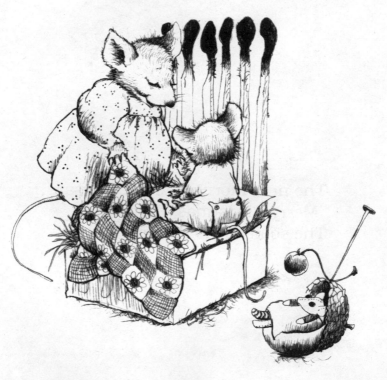

The next morning, someone says,
"Merry Christmas, Pippa."
The someone is Father.

"Merry Christmas," calls Someone Else.
The Someone Elses are Mother,
Ripple Squirrel, Gray Bird and Weber Duck.

"Merry Christmas, everyone," says Pippa.

Here is Pippa's Christmas tree.

Here is Pippa's swimming cap,
and here are some things in it—
many, many things.

Pippa puts on her swimming cap,
and plays with her Christmas things.

Then Pippa pulls some other things
out from behind her bed.

"Here is something for Mother and Father.

Here is something for Ripple Squirrel,

for Gray Bird and Weber Duck, too.
Hurray for Christmas," says Pippa.

Everyone plays a game,
everyone sings songs,
everyone sits down for Mother's dinner.

Then Pippa Mouse is sleepy.
"I would like Christmas
to last forever," says Pippa.

"What?" asks Father Mouse.
"And never have time to swim?
Or roll nuts?
Or run and play?
Or even try to fly?"

"Well," says Pippa,
"I want those times too.
But not right now.
Right now,
I don't want anything at all."

"Nothing at all, my Pippa?"
asks Mother.

"Yes, one thing," says Pippa.

"Right now, I want to go to sleep."

Pippa's Swim Day

The sun is very hot.
Bright and hot on Pippa's nose,
on Pippa's toes.

"Hurray for the swim day!" says Pippa Mouse.
She puts on her swimming cap
and runs down to the lake.

"Come for a swim with me," Pippa calls
to Gray Bird.

"Not me," says Gray Bird.
"Swimming is for fish, not for birds."
Gray Bird flies away.

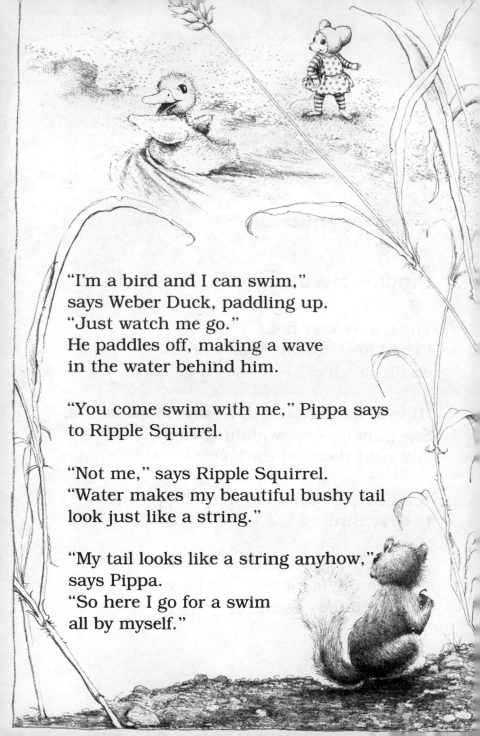

"I'm a bird and I can swim,"
says Weber Duck, paddling up.
"Just watch me go."
He paddles off, making a wave
in the water behind him.

"You come swim with me," Pippa says
to Ripple Squirrel.

"Not me," says Ripple Squirrel.
"Water makes my beautiful bushy tail
look just like a string."

"My tail looks like a string anyhow,"
says Pippa.
"So here I go for a swim
all by myself."

She runs down to the water and stops.
"Are you sure
you know how to swim, Pippa?"
asks Ripple Squirrel.

"How do I know?" asks Pippa.
"I haven't tried it yet."

She runs into the water a little way
and stops again.

"Weber Duck," calls Pippa.
"How do you swim?"

"I don't know how mice swim,"
says Weber. "But ducks swim like this:
They sit on top of the water,
push with their feet
and off they go."

"That looks easy," says Pippa.
"I can do that."

Pippa sits on top of the water.
But she doesn't stay on top of the water—
she goes under the water.

Pippa comes up, wiping her eyes.
"Mice don't swim like ducks," says Pippa.

"Well," says Weber, "maybe mice swim like fish.
Fish are swimming all the time."

Pippa bends over and looks at the minnows
swimming around and around by her toes.

"That looks easy," says Pippa.
"I can do that.
Fish just lie down,
and open and shut their mouths
without a sound.
They wiggle their tails
and swim round and around."

Pippa lies down in the water,
opens her mouth
and tries to wiggle her tail.
Down under the water again goes Pippa.
This time she swallows a lot of water.

She jumps up, wiping her eyes
and spitting out water.
When she can talk, Pippa says,
"Mice don't swim like fish.
And mice don't *want* to!
I'll find out how to swim all by myself!"

She shuts her mouth
and begins to paddle,
first with two paws, then
   with four paws.
Paddle, splash, splash.
Splash, paddle, splash.

"Look at me! Look at me!" yells Pippa.
"I'm swimming
with all four paws off the ground!"

Ripple Squirrel laughs.
She calls down to Pippa,
   "Fish swim with no feet,
   Ducks swim with two feet,
   But who swims with four feet
   Off the ground, all around?"

And proud paddling Pippa yells,
"Pippa Mouse, that's who!"

The Scary Faces Game

"Let's play the Scary Face game,"
Pippa Mouse says to her friends.

"All right," says Weber Duck.
"Look at my Scary Face."
He rolls his eyes and opens
his mouth very wide.

"That's not scary," says Gray Bird.
"Look at *my* Scary Face."
Gray Bird fluffs up her feathers,
blinks her eyes and snaps her beak very fast.

"That's not scary," says Ripple Squirrel.
"Look at my *very* Scary Face."
Ripple fluffs her big tail over her back,
and down over her nose.
Then she sticks her nose through her fluffy tail
and makes groaning noises.

"No, no," says Pippa Mouse.
"That's not a Scary Face.
Just look at my very, *very* Scary Face!"
Pippa Mouse crosses her eyes.
She pulls her mouth wide with her paws,
and shows all her teeth.
"Grrr!" says Pippa.

Ripple Squirrel laughs.
"Oh, Pippa," says Ripple.
"You're not scary at all!"

"No," says Gray Bird.
"You're too little to be scary!"

Weber Duck says,
"We could never be scared of you, Pippa."

"You *will* be scared of me," says Pippa.
"Just wait and see."

Pippa runs off
to find something to make her scary.
But there is nothing scary in the woods.

"Then I'll make something scary," says Pippa.
She makes a little green blanket
from dried grass, vine stems and old leaves.
Pippa pulls the blanket over her back
and looks at herself in a puddle.

But Pippa doesn't look scary at all.
She looks like a small mouse
in a little green blanket.

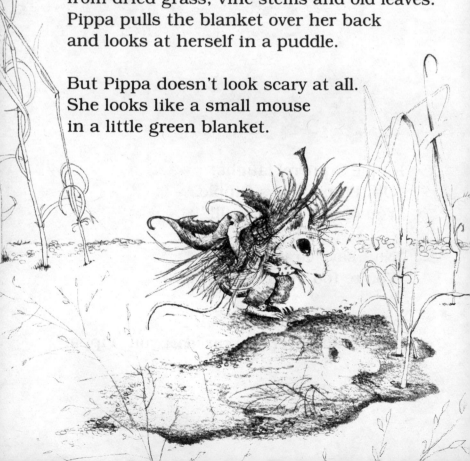

Then Pippa sees something silver
in the puddle.
An old piece of tin foil
in the muddy puddle.

She pulls it out,
pushes it flat
and pinches it into a hat.
Pippa puts the funny silver hat
on top of her head.
Only it doesn't stay on her head.
It slips down over her ears,
over her eyes,
right down to her toes.

75

"Now I'll run back and scare everybody,"
says Pippa.
Only Pippa can't run
because she can't see.
She can only look at the ground
down under her toes.

Bump. Pippa bumps into a stone.
Bumpity-bump. Pippa bumbles into a tree.

Bumping and bumbling along, Pippa calls,
"Here comes the hairy, scary Snipper-Bug,
snip-snapping through the woods."
Her voice sounds hollow and far away
under the big silver hat.

Old Owl is dozing in the tall oak tree.
Pippa's hollow calling wakes him up.
He opens his great round eyes
and sees something.

Owl spreads his wings and flies away.
He screeches, "Look out! Look out!
Here comes the Snipper-Bug!
The hairy, scary Snipper-Bug,
snip-snapping through the woods!"

Gray Bird flies to a branch.
Ripple runs up a tree.
And Weber Duck hides behind a rock.

All three keep very still. As still as a stone.

Then they see the Snipper-Bug
bumping into the tree
and bumbling into the rock.
They hear a funny hollow voice calling,
"Here comes the Snipper-Bug,
the hairy, scary Snipper-Bug,
snip-snapping through the woods!"

Gray Bird looks at the Snipper-Bug
with her bright black eyes.
She says, "That is not a Snipper-Bug,
that's a Pippa Mouse."

"Yes," says Ripple Squirrel.
"That funny little voice
is Pippa's voice."

"I knew it was you right away,"
says Gray Bird, flying down.
"You didn't scare us at all, Pippa."

Weber Duck waddles out.
He says, "Yes, Pippa did scare us.
She made us all hide."

"I guess I *was* scared—
just for a minute," says Gray Bird.

"Just at first," says Ripple,
"I was a little scared too."

"And Pippa scared Owl," says Weber.
"She made him fly away.
So Pippa wins the game."

Pippa pulls off the hat and laughs.
"You weren't really scared of *me*," she says.
"Neither was Old Owl.
You were all scared of the Snipper-Bug.
So the hairy, scary Snipper-Bug—and Pippa
win the Scary Faces game."

A Pet for Pippa

"I want a pet," says Pippa.
"A pet of my very own
to play with."

"A pet?" says Father Mouse.
"Who ever heard of a mouse with a pet?"

"You did," says Pippa.
"I just told you."

"A pet?" asks Mother.
"Where would you find a pet?"

"Somewhere," says Pippa.
"I'll go outside and look for a pet
right away."

The day outside is cold and gray.
All Pippa can hear
is the sound of leaves rustling
and a thin cricket song by the doorstep.

"I'll find a pet somewhere," says Pippa.

She walks and looks
and looks and walks.
Under a bit of fallen bark
she finds a furry caterpillar
curled up like a small woolly bear.

"Uncurl!" yells Pippa.
"Wake up and be my pet!"

But the woolly-bear caterpillar
doesn't uncurl
and he doesn't wake up.
He keeps right on sleeping.

A ladybug lands on Pippa's paw.
"Oh, Ladybug, you are just right
for a mouse's pet!" cries Pippa.

But the ladybug spreads her
spotted wings
and flies away.

Under a stone,
Pippa sees a big black beetle digging a hole.
Pippa grabs the beetle and tugs.
But the beetle tugs harder.
Pop! Over goes Pippa
and into his hole goes the beetle.

Pippa can't catch a spider or a brown moth either.
"But I *will* find a pet," says Pippa.

Then she hears someone scratching
in the dry ground leaves.
Scratch. Scritch. Scratch.

A big brown and red bird
is scratching among the leaves.

"Bird," says Pippa,
"will you please be my pet?"

The brown and red bird
looks down at Pippa.
"Silly mouse," he says.
"I am much too big
to be *your* pet.
But you are just the right size
for *my* pet. Climb on my back
and fly away South with me."

"No, no," says Pippa.
"I don't want to be your pet.
I want to have a pet of my own.
And I will find one."

"You'd better hurry up, then,"
says the big brown and red bird.
"The sun is getting low
and the night is closing in."

The bird flies away
and Pippa walks home
in the fading day.

"I will look for a pet tomorrow,"
says Pippa.
Then she stops by her doorstep
and listens.

What is that faint chirring sound?
It is the cricket still singing
by the doorstep.
Still singing a thin little cricket song.

Pippa bends down and says softly,
"Cricket, where are you?"

"Under your doorstep,"
a small voice says,
"trying to keep warm."

Pippa looks under the doorstep.
She sees a small green cricket
waving its feelers.

"Cricket," says Pippa,
"if you will live with me
and be my pet,
you will always be warm.
And have lots to eat."

"I don't know," says Cricket.
"Tell me first,
what *is* a pet?"

Pippa thinks.
Then she says,
"A pet is a friend,
a friend to take care of
and love."

"Good!" says Cricket.
"Then I will be *your* pet,
and you will be *my* pet.
Now tell me one thing more."

"What, Cricket?" asks happy Pippa.

Cricket says, "What time is supper?"

The Secret Hiding Place

Pippa Mouse has no one to play with.
"Everyone is too busy to play with me,"
says Pippa.

"Play with Cricket, then," says Father.
He and Mother Mouse are drying apples
for winter pies.

"Cricket is busy too," says Pippa.
"Too busy sleeping to play with me."

"Then," says Mother Mouse, "you must go
outside and play by yourself."

Pippa Mouse goes outside to play
by herself.
She tries to catch the falling leaves.
She pushes them
into a big pile
and jumps into it.

Run-jump. Run-jump.
The pile is all gone
and the leaves are all over the ground.

Then Pippa says, "I know what to do.
I'll find a secret hiding place
where no one can find me.
When they want to play with me,
they won't know where I am.
Then they'll be sorry. Very, very sorry."

Pippa runs through the woods
looking for a secret hiding place.

She finds a hole in the ground
just big enough for a small mouse
to squeeze into.
Push, wiggle, squeeze.
Pippa squeezes into the hole.

"Ouch!" yells Pippa.
"Someone pinched me!"

"I did," says Chipmunk.
"This is my house, Pippa.
Who asked you to come squeezing
and wiggling into my house
and messing it all up?"

"I thought it was a hiding hole,"
says Pippa.

"It is," says Chipmunk.
"*My* hiding hole.
Now go away, Pippa Mouse."

Pippa goes away.

She finds a good dry hiding place
between two big rocks.
"Only it hasn't any roof," says Pippa.

She pulls some branches and twigs
over the top of the rocks.
Then she covers them over with grass
and dry leaves.

"I will call this place P.S.H.P.
That will mean *Pippa's Secret Hiding Place*,"
says Pippa.
"I will hide here a long time.
Everyone will be very sorry
when they can't find Pippa."

Pippa hides in her secret hiding place.
She sits very still and waits.
And waits.

No one comes.
No friend calls, "Pippa, where are you?"
Pippa is very alone
in her secret hiding place.

"They can't find me," says Pippa.
"So I will go find them.
Maybe they are sorry enough by now."

Down by the lake
Pippa's friends are playing Tag.

"Hi, Pippa," calls Ripple Squirrel.

"Come play Tag," says Weber Duck.
"Our work is all done
and now it's time to play."

"Were you working too?"
says Gray Bird.

"Yes," says Pippa.
"I was making a surprise for you.
Come see it now."

Pippa takes her friends to P.S.H.P.
"That means *Pippa's Secret Hiding Place*,"
says Pippa.

Everyone crowds inside.

"This is a fine place," says Weber.

"Big enough for all of us,"
says Gray Bird.

"But it is J.F.P.," says Ripple.
"And that means *Just For Pippa*."

"No, no," says Pippa.
"It has a new name now.
Now it is E.S.H.P.
And that means *Everybody's Secret Hiding Place*
because it is for all of us!
And we will have a picnic here
this very afternoon!"

The Tracks in the Snow

Snow!
On the tree branches,
on the mouse-house roof,
and all over the ground.

Pippa Mouse pulls on her snow things
and runs outside.

She jumps in the snow
and rolls in the snow
and throws snow high in the air.

"Snow, cold snow," sings Pippa.
"Where do you come from?
Where do you go?"

Pippa makes a big snowmouse.
Then she throws snowballs at it.
She makes snow pictures with a stick,
and eats a snowcake.

"Where is everyone?" asks Pippa.
"Why don't they come out
and play in the snow?
I'll go find them."

Pippa doesn't find *them.*
But she does find some tracks in the snow.
"I will follow my friends," Pippa says.
"I will track them in the snow."

Pippa follows the tracks
through the trees,
around the rocks,
over the deep cold snow.
She finds Gray Bird, Ripple and Weber
together high on the hill.

"Look out!" calls Pippa.
"Something is following me!
See the wiggling tracks in the snow?
Maybe it is a snake-thing
trying to catch me!"

"Silly Pippa Mouse,"
says Ripple Squirrel.
"That is not a snake-thing
coming after you."

"That is the track
of your very own tail!"
Gray Bird says.
"It's following you in the snow!"

"Come slide down the hill with us,"
says Weber Duck.

Up and down the hill they go,
on some bits of tree bark.
Fast down and up slow
they go,
until the shadows creep up the hill
and the sun is red and low.

"I'm as cold as ice," says Gray Bird.
"Let's go home."

"My stomach is saying 'suppertime,' "
says Weber Duck.

"Come on, Pippa," Ripple Squirrel says.
"What are you looking at?"

I'm looking at these tracks," says Pippa.
"Who made these tracks in the snow?
They're not your tracks, Ripple.
They're not your tracks, Gray Bird.
You did not make these tracks, Weber Duck."

"They are not your tracks, Pippa,"
says Ripple Squirrel.

"They are not even the tracks
of your long mouse tail."

"No," says Pippa.
"They are fine big paw prints
of a big Red Fox,
who is not very far away!"

Quick as a wink
            quick as a sneeze
                        quick as a fox
Ripple, Gray Bird, Weber and Pippa
run home
through the deep white snow.

"Well, Pippa Mouse," says Father.
"For once, you are home early,
just in time for your supper.
Were you tired of playing in the snow?"

"No," says Pippa Mouse,
sitting close to the warm red fire.
"Only some tracks in the snow
told me it was time to go."

Pippa's Party

Today is Pippa's birthday.
Before the sun is up,
Pippa is up.
"I'm too wiggly to stay in bed,"
says Pippa.
"I feel too fizzy inside."

"Happy Birthday, Pippa,"
says Cricket.
He hops into Pippa's room
carrying something in his small jaws.
Something wrapped up in a green leaf.

"Here is a birthday present," says Cricket.
"I found it blowing around in the wind."

Pippa unwraps the green leaf.
Inside she finds some fluffy white stuff.
"What is it, Cricket?" she asks.

Cricket says, "I don't know.
But maybe you could use it for
making snowflakes,
or whiskers or a fluffy white tail."

"It is a good present, Cricket," says Pippa.
"My very first present
on my birthday."

Mother and Father Mouse come in the room.
They are carrying a toy mouse in a toy house.
"We made them for you, Pippa," they say.
"Happy Birthday, dear Pippa!"

Pippa Mouse gives everyone
a big birthday hug.
Then she sits down
to play with the toy mouse in the toy house.

"What will you name your mouse?"
asks Cricket.

Pippa says, "I will call him Teeni-Mouse.
Teeni-Mouse in his own Teeni-House.
And I will play with him all day."

"Not *all* day, Pippa," says Father.
"Let's eat breakfast first."

"Not *all* day, Pippa," says Mother.
"For this afternoon
is your birthday party!
All your friends are coming."

"And bringing me presents too,"
says Pippa, "I think."

After breakfast, Pippa says,
"Cricket, we can't play right now.
I have to tell my friends
something important.
Something very important."

Pippa finds her friends, Weber,
Ripple and Gray Bird, down by the lake.

"Hi!" calls Pippa.
"I have something important to tell you.
Did you know
when people come to a birthday party
they should bring presents
for the birthday mouse?"

"Oh, Pippa," says Ripple.
"We already know that."

"You told us that yesterday,"
says Weber Duck.

"And the day before yesterday too,"
says Gray Bird.

"I thought maybe you might forget,"
says Pippa.
"I didn't want you to be surprised."

Ripple Squirrel says,
"We will surprise *you*, Pippa Mouse!
For we are going to dress up
in costumes for your party.
Your mother said we could."

"Oh," says Pippa.
Then she says, "Come on, Cricket.
We can't stand here talking all morning.
A birthday is a very busy day.
We have important things to do."

"What important things?" asks Cricket,
hopping along beside Pippa.

"We have to think
of costumes for us
to dress up in," says Pippa.

"What costumes?" asks Cricket.

"I don't know," says Pippa.
"We must think very hard!"

In Pippa's room
they sit down to think.

Cricket begins to play
with Teeni-Mouse.

"No, no, Cricket," says Pippa.
"Think. Think hard!"

They think some more.
"Are you thinking hard, Cricket?" asks Pippa.

Cricket is not thinking hard.
Cricket is not thinking at all.
Cricket is asleep.

"Wake up, wake up!" Pippa calls,
shaking Cricket awake.
"You don't have to think anymore.
I know how we'll dress up."

Soon Mother and Father Mouse
hear a knocking on the mouse-house door.

Father opens the door and says,
"Come in, Gray Bird and Ripple
and Weber Duck."

"I am not Gray Bird. I am Gray Witch,"
says Gray Bird.

"I am not Weber. I am Dr. Duck," says Weber.

Ripple Squirrel says, "And I am Super-Squirrel!"

"Glad to meet you," says Father.
"You are just in time for the birthday party."

"But where is Pippa?" asks Gray Bird.
"I don't see the birthday mouse anywhere."

"Here she is!" says Pippa,
popping into the room.
"Only now her name is Little Bo-Pippa
who lost her sheep.
And here is the sheep."

A small Something covered with white fluff
hops into the room.

"Oh, Pippa," says Ripple.
"That's really Cricket.
But he's a very good sheep, too."

Pippa says, "Did you forget to bring . . .?"

"No, no, don't say it!" says Weber.
"Here are your presents, Little Bo-Pippa."

Everyone says, "Happy Birthday, Pippa."
Pippa opens her presents and everyone plays
with them. Then they play birthday games
like *Jump-Mouse, Weber's Bridge Is Falling
Down* and *Pin the Tail on the Squirrel.*

When they are tired,
they sit down to eat.
They have maple sugar ice with sassafras sauce,
Father Mouse's famous flapjacks,
and candy corn cookies.
Last of all, Mother Mouse brings in
a beautiful acorn cake,
all bright with birthday candles.

Everyone sings, "Happy Birthday, Dear Pippa."
And loudest of all, Pippa Mouse sings,
"Happy Birthday, Dear Me!"

BETTY BOEGEHOLD was active in elementary education for many years. She was also a writer, editor, and graduate instructor at New York's Bank Street College of Education—specializing in beginning-reader materials.

CYNDY SZEKERES is well known for her irresistible animal characters. She lives with her family on a farm in Vermont.